W9-BJU-039

Can't You Make Them Behave, King George?

by Jean Fritz

pictures by Tomie de Paola

PAPERSTAR

G. P. Putnam's Sons

The Putnam & Grosset Group

Text copyright © 1977 by Jean Fritz
Illustrations copyright © 1977 by Tomie dePaola
All rights reserved. This book, or parts thereof,
may not be reproduced in any form without permission
in writing from the publisher. PaperStar and G. P. Putnam's Sons
are divisions of The Putnam & Grosset Group,
200 Madison Avenue, New York, NY 10016.
PaperStar is a registered trademark of The Putnam Berkley Group, Inc.
The PaperStar logo is a trademark of The Putnam Berkley Group, Inc.
Originally published in 1977 by Coward McCann, Inc.
First PaperStar edition published in 1996
Published simultaneously in Canada
Printed in the United States of America

Library of Congress Cataloging-in-Publication Data
Fritz, Jean. Can't you make them behave, King George?
Summary: A biography of George the Third, King of Great Britain
at the time of the American Revolution. I. George III,
King of Great Britain, 1738-1820—Juvenile literature.
I. dePaola, Thomas Anthony. II. Title
DA506.A2F74   1976   941.07'3'0924 [B] 75-33722
ISBN 0-399-23304-0 (hardcover)
20 19 18 17 16 15 14
PaperStar ISBN 0-698-11402-7 (paperback)
10 9 8 7 6

To Margaret Swart
—*J.F.*

For Margot Tomes
—*T. de P.*

Before King George the Third was either king or the Third, he was just plain George, a bashful boy who blushed easily. His toes turned in when he walked, and his teachers nagged him about being lazy. Now, of course, as everyone knows, a king should not blush or turn in his toes or be lazy, but George didn't think much about being a king. His grandfather, George the Second, was king at the moment, and when he died, George's father, Frederick, would be king. And not until Frederick died would George have to worry about his turn.

So he went on blushing and turning in his toes. He daydreamed and sometimes drew pictures on the margins of his school papers. Once after a scolding he put tar on a teacher's seat so that when the teacher sat down, he had a hard time getting up.

GEORGE!

Then suddenly on March 20, 1751, when George was 12 years old, his father died. And George, instead of being just plain George, was George, Prince of Wales. The next king. What was more, everyone expected George to start behaving like the next king. *Right now*.

"Take your elbows off the table, George," his mother would say. "Be a *king!*

"Don't gobble your food, George. Do you want to look like your Uncle Cumberland?

"Stand up straight, George. Kings don't slouch."

He was surrounded by private tutors, who from morning to night gave him arithmetic problems to solve, history lessons to learn, Latin passages to translate. They told him to turn out his toes, to speak up, to keep still, to be a man, to get to work. Sometimes George sulked under so much instruction. Once after a particularly hard Latin passage written by an old Roman named Caesar, George wrote on his paper: "Mr. Caesar, I wish you would go to the devil." But for the most part he tried to do what he was told. He paid particular attention to his favorite tutor, Lord Bute, who seemed to know all the rules for the king business. And since he was going to have to be king, George decided that when the time came, he would be a good one. He would be a father to his people.

The time came on October 25, 1760, when George was 22 years old. His grandfather died, and suddenly there was George, all by himself, the new king. The first thing he did was to gallop off to see Lord Bute and check the rules. If he was going to be a good king, he wanted to start off right.

And he did. He even looked like a king—tall, auburn-haired, with well-shaped legs and toes going the right direction. (Occasionally he had pimples, people noticed, but never more than one or two at a time.) When he made a speech, he stood straight and spoke in a strong voice. At parties he didn't just stare at

RULE ONE...

the floor, as his grandfather had done, he mixed with his company, and he didn't just hold out his hand for ladies to kiss, he kissed the ladies.

John Hancock, who was visiting London, wrote back to America: The new king was good-natured and well liked.

But of course, what a king needed was a queen, and George the Third refused to be crowned until he had a queen to be crowned with him. He sent scouts scurrying to Europe to find out what princesses were available. There turned out to be seven princesses.

One princess was fond of philosophy, and the king said he didn't want that. One was too young; two were stubborn; one had a grandfather who had married a druggist's daughter; one had a mother who had been in jail. The king said no to all of them. At the bottom of the list was 16-year-old Princess Charlotte of Mecklenburg (a state in north Germany). Princess Charlotte had rather a large mouth, but otherwise the king could find nothing wrong with her. So he said yes, and she said yes, and he made the plans.

First, the king sent for the princess' measurements. Then he supervised the making of her wedding dress. It was to be a silver and white gown with a mantle of violet velvet lined with ermine and fastened on one shoulder with a bunch of pearls. He ordered a diamond tiara, and he had the royal yacht repainted and renamed the *Charlotte*. He picked out 11 bridesmaids and ordered their clothes. Indeed there was no detail that the king did not see to, even though in the midst of preparations, he came down with chicken pox.

Meanwhile, Princess Charlotte, who didn't want to leave home at all, picked all the herbs in her private herb garden and all the flowers in her private flower garden, and she gave them away to the poor. She practiced playing "God Save the King" on her harpsichord and learned to sing the words. Since she didn't speak English, this was not easy, but she practiced and practiced. She even practiced on the royal yacht crossing the North Sea when everyone else in her party was too seasick to sit up.

Princess Charlotte and King George met at 3 in the afternoon of September 8, 1761, and they were married at 9 the same evening. The princess' wedding dress fit all right, but the king had counted too much on that bunch of pearls. The ermine mantle was so heavy that she had a hard time keeping the dress on her shoulders. But she said, "I do," and he said, "I do." Then they went to the palace, and Charlotte sang and played "God Save the King" for the royal family.

Now for the crowning. On September 22, King George and Queen Charlotte rode in sedan chairs to Westminster Abbey to be crowned by the Archbishop of Canterbury. At the beginning of the ceremony the archbishop cried out, "I here present unto you George, the undoubted king of the realm." Everyone in the abbey shouted, "God save the king!" Then the archbishop turned to all four points of the compass—north, south, east, west—and each time presented George, the undoubted king. Each time the people responded, "God save the king!"

George and Charlotte put on the royal robes, received the royal regalia, made the promises they had to make, and finally the coronation was over. George had a crown on his head and felt like a real king. Not only father to the thousands of people who were cheering outside the abbey, but a father to all the people in his whole empire, including the men, women, and children in faraway America.

Indeed King George was feeling so good that he seemed hardly to mind the things that went wrong at his coronation banquet.

First were the candles. Lord Talbot, the king's chief steward, thought how clever it would be if suddenly all the 2,000 candles in the banquet hall could light up at the same time just as the king, queen, and the guests came into the room. So he had the candles connected with a string of flax fuses, and when the people entered, he lighted the flax and the candles burst into flame just as he had planned. What he had not planned was that the burning flax would turn into thousands of sparks and shower down on the heads of those present. (The ladies screamed, but no one was hurt.)

Then the chairs. Lord Talbot forgot to provide chairs for the king and queen, and since no one could sit down until the king and queen did, there was a great deal of standing about until the proper chairs were found. And when at last people could sit, there were not enough tables for them to sit at. No table for the Lord Mayor of London and the aldermen. So they were moved to the table reserved for the Knights of the Bath, and the Knights of the Bath were crowded in among the law lords. Then because Lord Talbot thought he would be clever and save money, there wasn't enough food to go around. When some barons complained, Lord Talbot asked them if they wanted to fight.

Worst of all was the horse ceremony. Lord Talbot was supposed to ride his horse into the banquet hall and up to the king and queen to pay his official respects. In preparing for the ceremony, Lord Talbot thought how clever it would be if his horse, instead of turning around, would back away from the king and queen. For days he trained his horse to walk backward, and at the banquet that was just what it did. But instead of walking forward to the king and queen and *then* backing away, the horse backed its rear end right up to the king and queen.

Anyway, mistakes or not, George the Third was king, and now what? Well, he had to be a good king. So he set about following the rules.

A king, his mother told him, should not be fat. So he tried not to eat much. Fresh fruit and sauerkraut were his favorite foods. (Sometimes his guests thought he didn't want them to be fat either. Once a friend reported that after a whole day of hunting with the king, of galloping and leaping, of being popped into ditches and jerked over gates, what do you think the king offered him? A little barley water!)

Next, a king must be moral. So at once King George issued a royal proclamation against the use of bad language.

Furthermore, a king should not break promises. Once King George was thrown from a horse and was so black and blue that his doctors wanted to keep him in bed. But he had promised to go to the theater that night. So up he got and off he went. A promise was a promise, he said.

And of course, a king should have heirs. This took a little longer, but over the years King George and Queen Charlotte had 15 children: George, Frederick, William, Charlotte, Edward, Augusta, Elizabeth, Ernest, Augustus, Adolphus, Mary, Sophia, Octavius, Alfred, and Amelia. Once a week the family walked in pairs around the garden so the public could view them. (Princess Augusta hated this.)

Another rule was that a king should be orderly. This was not hard for George; he loved order—everything in its proper place, everyone at his own work. He liked to walk around the countryside and see that even the land was doing its job. (He didn't like mountains. Useless things, he called them.)

And he was exact. If he said dinner was at eight, he meant *exactly* at eight. When he measured the height of the princes, he measured it to a sixteenth of an inch. When he dated a letter, he included not only the day and the year, but the hour and the minute that he started writing.

In addition, a king should be careful of money. So instead of having satin or velvet curtains around his bed, King George made do with plain white cotton ones. He refused to have a rug on his bedroom floor (it would be unmanly, he said), and except on public occasions he dressed plainly. He personally inspected the kitchen to make sure that there was no waste, and in order to cut down on the number of servants, he had the queen's hairdresser serve meals.

Of course, concerned as he was about household costs, the king was also concerned about government costs, and when George came to the throne, the government was costing a great deal. England had been fighting a long and expensive war, and when it was over, the question was how to pay the bills. Finally, a government official suggested that one way to raise money was to tax Americans.

"What a good idea!" King George said. After all, the French and Indian part of the war had been fought on American soil for the benefit of Americans, so why shouldn't they help pay for it? The fact that Americans had also spent money and lost men in the war didn't seem important. Nor did the fact that Americans had always managed their own money up to now. They were English subjects, weren't they? Didn't English subjects have to obey the English government? So in 1765 a stamp tax was laid on certain printed items in America.

King George was amazed that Americans objected. He was flabbergasted that they claimed he had no *right* to tax them. Just because they had no say in the matter. Just because they had no representatives in the English government. What was more, Americans refused to pay. If they agreed to one tax, they said, what would come next? A window tax? A tax on fireplaces?

Now King George believed that above all a king should be firm, but the government had the vote, and in the end it voted to repeal the tax. Still, King George was pleased about one thing: The government stood firm on England's *right* to tax the colonies. And in 1767 the government tried again. This time the tax was on lead, tea, paint, and a number of items England sold to America. Part of the money from this tax was to be used to support an English army to keep order in America; part was to pay governors and judges previously under the control of the colonies. Who could object to that? King George asked.

The Americans did. They hated the whole business so much, especially the English soldiers stationed in their midst, that even when the other taxes were repealed and only the tea tax remained, they would not put up with it. When tea arrived in Boston, they dumped it into Boston Harbor.

When he heard this news, King George felt more like a father than he ever had in his life. A father with a family of very, very disobedient children. And of course, he must punish them. So he closed the port of Boston and took away the right of Massachusetts to govern itself.

Firm, firm, firm. From now on he would be firm. After the Battle of Lexington and the Battle of Bunker Hill, King George said he felt strong as a lion. People would soon see, he said, that Americans would back down, meek as lambs.

Instead, on July 4, 1776, Americans declared their independence. Naturally King George was annoyed. But he wasn't worried. How could children, however rebellious, succeed against a firm father? How could a few colonies hold out against a powerful empire? He'd just send a few more regiments over and then watch the Americans come around! It never occurred to George the Third that he might not be right. "I wish nothing but good," he once said, "therefore everyone who does not agree with me is a traitor or a scoundrel."

For a while King George had every reason to feel confident. The English troops captured New York, and when George heard this, he said one more battle and it would be over. When he was told that his troops had marched into Philadelphia, he ran into the queen's room. "I have beat them!" he shouted. "Beat all the Americans!"

But he hadn't beaten them. The fighting went on, and meanwhile, George the Third had to go about the business of being a king. He put his seal on official papers, gave out medals and titles, memorized the name of every ship in the navy, tasted the food sent to the troops, checked on who was spending what, and for hours on end he listened to people talk.

Indeed, being a king, especially a good king, was often boring. He couldn't even drop a glove without half the palace, it seemed, stooping to pick it up and arguing about who should have the honor of returning it. "Never mind the honor," the king once said. "Never mind, never mind. Just give me my glove. What? what? what? Yes, you all picked it up, yes, yes, yes, all, all, all—you all picked it up." (King George had a habit of talking rapidly and repeating himself so that his talk often sounded like a gobble.)

But as king, he did have a few advantages. He was, for instance, the most prayed-for man in the empire. Naturally it was pleasant to think of the heavy traffic of prayers ascending on his behalf every Sunday morning. From every country church and every city cathedral in every corner of the kingdom. (But not in America. There the preachers gave up praying for him when the Punishment started.) The king was also the most toasted man. No party (except in America) began without all the people present raising their glasses and wishing the king a long life. (The king wished it, too.) And he had the biggest birthday celebration. Each year on June 4 all his subjects (except in America, of course) celebrated his birthday with parades and banquets and speeches and gunfire and fireworks.

All those prayers and toasts and fireworks were not to be sneezed at. Still, there were times when George wanted to forget about being a king. Fortunately he had hobbies to turn to. For one thing, he made metal buttons (he loved turning a lathe). He wrote articles on farming and signed himself "Ralph Richardson" which was the name of one of his shepherds. He played backgammon with the officers of the royal household, and he collected ship models, coins, clocks, and watches. (He had a four-sided clock that even showed the tides.) He played the flute and harpsichord, hunted, and studied the stars in his private observatory. And for the queen's special amusement, he maintained a zoo, which consisted of one elephant and one zebra.

But always in the end he had to go back to being a king. Back to the problem of America. This was the way he thought of America. A problem. King George did not really think of the Revolutionary War as a *war* until the fall of 1777, when 5,000 English soldiers surrendered to the Americans at Saratoga.

How could such a thing happen? the king asked. Hadn't he been told, even by an ex-governor of Massachusetts, that Americans would give up? That only a small number of Americans were really against him? And how could he, a peace-loving king, find himself in an honest-to-goodness war with his own colonies? He tried to console himself. He was a good king, he said. Good kings deserve to win. So this must be a temporary setback. All he had to do was to show the world that he wasn't the least bit worried. So that night after hearing about the defeat, King George went to a court party and spent the evening telling stupid jokes and laughing so uproariously that his Prime Minister, Lord North, had to take him aside and try to quiet him down.

The war dragged on. France, impressed with the victory at Saratoga, joined the war on America's side. There were people in England now who wanted to stop fighting, but not George. No, no, no. Never, never. No independence. No peace without honor. If one group of English colonies got away, what would happen to the others? What would be left of the empire?

But no matter how he showed himself in public, privately George was depressed. The world was not staying settled, everything in place, the way he liked it. Not only was America acting up, but there were difficulties in England as well. Riots even. And George's own family was misbehaving. Two of his brothers were involved in scandals, and George's son, the Prince of Wales, was so contrary he deliberately arrived for meals as much as an hour late although he *knew* that the king wanted everyone to be *exactly* on time.

On November 25, 1781, the news reached London that the English army under General Cornwallis had surrendered at Yorktown to General Washington. When Lord North heard this, he threw up his arms. "It's all over!" he said.

But the king said nothing was over. They still had ships, hadn't they? (He named them.) They still had officers. (He had learned their names, too.) They still had troops. They still had guns and gunpowder.

King George set his lips firmly and wrote a letter to the Secretary of State for America. This defeat, he said, should not make the smallest difference in their plans. Still, King George was so upset that when he dated the letter, he forgot to record the hour and the minute of the writing.

Two days later the king addressed the government.
"I prohibit you from thinking of peace," he thundered.

But the government did think of peace, and eventually the government voted for it.

So now what? King George couldn't fight the war all by himself. He couldn't chop off the heads of all those who had voted for peace. Kings didn't do that anymore. He could, of course, abdicate—quit the king business altogether. For a time he thought seriously of this. He even drafted an announcement of his abdication, but then he put it away in his desk. He was so *used* to being a king. So when the time came for him to sign the peace proclamation, he signed. As soon as he had finished, he jumped on his horse and took a hard gallop away from the palace. When the time came to announce in public the separation of the two countries and the independence of America, he swallowed hard and announced. Afterward he asked a friend if he had spoken loudly enough.

As long as he lived, King George had nightmares about the loss of the American colonies. It certainly hadn't been his fault, he said. *He* hadn't done anything wrong. He had just wanted to teach Americans a lesson. Give them all bloody noses—that's what he'd wanted.

Page 9 George wrote his wish for "Mr. Caesar" in French: You can see in his original scrawl just how disgusted he was.

Page 31 Americans also contended that if they had been *asked* (instead of being forced) to raise money for England, they would have done so as they had done on previous occasions.

In King George's day the king was a "constitutional monarch." He had lost the enormous powers that a king had once had and had to abide by the vote of the government. On the other hand, unlike present kings, he took an active and leading role in the government.

Page 32 Many Americans disapproved of the Boston Tea Party. They were willing to pay for the lost tea, but when instead the king punished them so severely, they became more united against him.

Page 47 In 1788 when the king was 50 years old, he became violently ill of a disease that has since been diagnosed as porphyria. One of the symptoms of the disease is that one's mind is affected, but in those days people thought that the king had simply gone mad. He recovered from his first attack but in later years suffered again. For the last ten years of his life he was a wretched-looking figure dressed in a purple bathrobe with wild white hair and a wild white beard. He died in 1820 at the age of 82.